CONTENTS

ADVENTURES IN WILD SPACE

THE HEIST

As the evil Emperor Palpatine strengthens his iron grip on the galaxy, Lina and Milo Graf search for their missing parents, kidnapped by Captain Korda of the Imperial Navy.

Traveling on board the WHISPER BIRD with their trusted droid, CR-8R, the children have learned the source of a mysterious transmission that is calling for a rebellion against the Empire itself. Their course is set for the planet Lothal.

Little do Lina and Milo know that sinister forces are closing in, greedy for the secret information lodged in CR-8R's memory banks. . . .

STAR WARS

ADVENTURES IN WILD SPACE

THE HEIST

CAVAN SCOTT

PRESS

LOS ANGELES · NEW YORK

© & TM 2017 Lucasfilm Ltd.

All rights reserved. Published by Disney · Lucasfilm Press, an imprint of
Disney Book Group. No part of this book may be reproduced or transmitted
in any form or by any means, electronic or mechanical, including photocopying,
recording, or by any information storage and retrieval system,
without written permission from the publisher.
For information address Disney · Lucasfilm Press,
1101 Flower Street, Glendale, California 91201.
Printed in the United States of America
First United States Paperback Edition, April 2017
1 3 5 7 9 10 8 6 4 2
FAC-029261—17067
ISBN 978-1-368-00314-8
Library of Congress Control Number: 2016942980

Cover art by Lucy Ruth Cummins
Interior art by David Buisán

Visit the official *Star Wars* website at: www.starwars.com.

SUSTAINABLE
FORESTRY
INITIATIVE

Certified Chain of Custody
Promoting Sustainable Forestry
www.sfiprogram.org
SFI-01054
The SFI label applies to the text stock

CHAPTER 1
SHADY BUSINESS

CAPTAIN KORDA scowled at the viewport in front of him. The swirling crimson eye of a gas giant stared back.

To Korda's right, an Imperial officer nervously approached him, holding out a datapad.

"Captain, we have the latest findings for you."

He was a pathetic-looking young man, with a fleshy, pockmarked face and a belly that strained against his gray uniform.

"And you are?" Korda snapped.

The young officer swallowed. "Junior Lieutenant Jams, sir."

Korda snatched the pad from the junior lieutenant's shaking hand.

"Your uniform is a disgrace, Jams. Those boots look like they haven't been cleaned in months, your collar is filthy, and your insignia is crooked."

Jams looked nervously down at the rank plaque on his chest, two red squares sitting atop two blue ones. He lifted his large hand to adjust the pins but hesitated, thinking better of it.

"I'm sorry, sir. I'll do better next time."

"Make sure that you do," Korda growled, slapping the datapad against Jams's chest. "If you come onto my bridge looking like that again, you'll wish you never went to the Imperial Academy."

"Yes, sir," Jams stuttered, almost dropping the pad before he scurried off. "Thank you, sir."

Korda sighed. How had it come to this? Not long before he had been the rising star of the Imperial Navy. He'd received medals of honor from Governor Tarkin and been given missions by Lord Vader himself. Now he was cataloging the locations of gas giants on the edge of Wild Space in a rundown freighter. He was constantly bored. His days were filled with pointless scans and tedious reports. Even bullying his pathetic excuse for a crew had lost its joy.

He rubbed the skin around his metal jaw. The scarred flesh itched terribly, another reminder of his failure. All this disgrace was down to two children—Lina and Milo Graf. It had seemed like such a simple mission at the time: arrest cartographers Auric and Rhyssa Graf and confiscate their extensive archive of planetary maps. How could he have known that Rhyssa would trick them by hiding the data in a droid? Or that the two Graf brats and the droid would evade capture so skillfully? Korda could still hear Lord Vader's words when he'd reported the news.

"You let *children* escape?"

Korda had been lucky to get out of the briefing with his life.

He would not stand for any of this. He wouldn't spend the rest of his career out there, wasting away in the farthest reaches of space.

He marched across the bridge, only to find his path blocked by an ensign with dark skin and a worried expression.

"Sir, we are scheduled for another seven hours around Klytus V . . ." he said.

Korda stepped around the young officer, heading for the doors. "Then you won't be needing me, Ensign. I'll expect a full report at the end of your shift. Do you understand?"

"Yes, sir," the ensign replied as Korda stormed from the bridge.

Korda walked into his private quarters and locked the door behind him. He pulled off his hat and threw it across the cramped cabin onto the bed. Sitting in front of a tiny holo-projector, he tapped his private access code into the computer and opened the secret comms-channel he'd been using for the past few weeks.

If he was going to restore his reputation, he needed to take action—fast.

The holo-projector beeped as it established a connection, piggybacking Korda's signal on an official Imperial communication.

Finally, after what seemed like an eternity, a translucent image appeared in the air before Korda. The captain found himself looking into the glowing eyes of a masked figure, who scowled back at him from beneath a heavy hood.

"Captain, this is not a convenient time," the figure said sharply.

"I've told you not to use my rank on an open channel," Korda snapped back. "And I'll decide whether it's convenient or not."

The hologram inclined its head. "Of course, sir."

That's better, Korda thought. It was about time he was given the respect he deserved.

"What have you discovered?" he asked.

"I am following a lead."

This is like pulling teeth from a bantha, Korda thought. "Where?"

"That doesn't concern you."

"Doesn't concern me? I'm the one paying you!"

"And the reason my fee is so high is that you insisted on complete discretion. After all, a respected Imperial officer hiring a bounty hunter? What would your superiors think?"

Korda struggled to keep his temper in check. The bounty hunter was mocking him, but he was also right. Korda was breaking every rule in the book by employing the Shade, one of the most notorious mercenaries in the Outer Rim. But it would be worth it. If the Shade could find the Grafs' maps, Korda could use the data to make a series of incredible discoveries in Wild Space. High Command would welcome him back with open arms if he unearthed a new energy source or a cache of precious metal.

And if he got rid of the pesky Graf children in the process, well then so be it.

"Very well. I'll expect a report—"

"Understood," the Shade interrupted him, terminating the connection. The hologram vanished, leaving Korda fuming in silence.

Once he was back where he belonged, he would take great pleasure in executing the bounty hunter in the Emperor's name.

＜━━➤

Thousands of light-years away, the Shade slapped shut a wrist-mounted holo-receiver.

The bounty hunter stepped off of a shabby porch and looked up and down the narrow alley. It was empty, although the sounds of the neighboring street could be heard. This was Skree, a century-old space station hidden in the middle of a dust nebula. Away from the Empire's prying eyes, it housed some of the worst scum in the galaxy. The Shade felt right at home.

The cloaked bounty hunter swept down the alley. It was almost time for the rendezvous. Reaching a corner, the Shade peeked around and spotted a tall alien named Meggin. He had taken the Shade's bait—the promise of a lead on the whereabouts of the alien's treasure-loving boss, Gozetta. Perfect.

Looking around nervously, Meggin walked into a rundown restaurant. That was the Shade's cue. The bounty hunter crossed the busy street, following Meggin into the crumbling building. The alien was inside, looking around in confusion. The restaurant was empty—just as the Shade had arranged for it to be.

Meggin turned, his small sunken eyes widening as he saw the black sphere in the

Shade's gloved hand. With a flick of the bounty hunter's wrist, the sphere shot through the air toward Meggin, hitting the alien in the chest. It pinned him to the wall like a Sriluurian butterfly that had been mounted on a board.

"You can struggle as much as you like," the Shade sneered, stalking forward. "But you're trapped in a localized force field. Not even a gundark could break free of its grip."

"W-what do you want?" Meggin stammered.

"Information," came the reply. A hologram of two children filled the air. "Milo and Lina Graf—where are they?"

Meggin shook his head. "I don't know who they are!"

"That's a lie," the Shade said calmly. "Now, let's try this again."

The mercenary pushed a button on the wrist-mounted comlink. Meggin cried out in pain as the metal orb pressed harder into his chest.

"I've just increased the gravitational pressure of the sphere. It will continue to crush you until you tell the truth," the Shade explained.

Still, the red-skinned alien refused to answer. The Shade pressed the control again, and Meggin gasped in discomfort. The Shade smiled cruelly. It was only a matter of time before the alien talked.

―――

Fifteen minutes later, the Shade strode out of the building. The bounty hunter had gotten his answer and was already planning the fastest route to the Outer Rim.

The Graf children were heading to Lothal, and the Shade would be waiting for them.

CHAPTER 2
LOTHAL

LINA GRAF SAT back in the *Whisper Bird*'s pilot seat and looked at the blue-and-green planet that lay ahead of them.

So that was Lothal.

It looked so peaceful, with clouds swirling across its surface. She had almost forgotten what peacefulness felt like. Her life had been turned upside down in the past week. Ever since the Galactic Empire had captured her parents, Lina and her brother, Milo, had escaped stormtroopers, TIE fighters, and ferocious creatures. No wonder she felt so tired. Right now, all she wanted was to roll up in a ball and go to sleep. But that wouldn't help them find their parents.

The navicomputer beeped. The *Whisper Bird* would be entering Lothal's atmosphere within a few minutes.

At least the ship was operating properly for once. The *Bird* had always been temperamental. It was held together by a mixture of obsolete gear and luck but had taken a real beating over the past few days. Lina had pushed the hyperdrive to the limits and every system had seemed to be on the verge of collapse. She glanced at the fault locator on the central console. No lights were flashing. No alarms sounding. Maybe that was why she felt uneasy. Was she getting used to exploding circuits and emergency repairs?

The journey to Lothal had been surprisingly free of crisis. They had dropped Sata and Meggin off in the Skree nebula and followed the signal of the transmission they had first picked up on Thune.

Lina's fingers ran along the comms-control as she tried to find the frequency, hidden among official Imperial communications. At first there was static, but then she heard a snatch of the now familiar voice. It was a man, speaking close to a microphone.

"They say they have our best interests at heart, but it's not true. Every day more people vanish. The Empire is lying to us. They are—"

The voice was lost in a burst of white noise as the connection broke. It didn't matter. Meggin had told Lina and Milo that the transmissions came from Lothal's Capital City. Maybe whoever was making the broadcasts could help them find their parents—or might know someone who could.

It was a long shot, but they were running out of options.

Lina pushed the *Whisper Bird*'s engines just a little harder.

They were almost there.

Somewhere behind her, there was a loud crash followed by an electronic wail.

"Milo?" Lina cried out, jumping out of her

seat and racing from the cockpit. "What was that? Is it the gravity compensators? Have they overloaded?"

The only answer she received was a sharp yell from her younger brother. "Look out!"

"Milo?"

She barreled into the living quarters and ducked as something large zoomed overhead.

In front of her, Milo was rolling on the floor, laughing hysterically!

She ducked again as the heavy object swept past her head. It was their droid, CR-8R, his repulsors firing.

"Get it off me!" the droid screeched as he banged against the far wall.

"Get what off you?" Lina asked before spotting the wiry Kowakian monkey-lizard clamped around the droid's head. The small creature was cackling as CR-8R tried to pry it off with flailing arms.

"Morq!" Lina yelled. The monkey-lizard

turned his head to stare at her. He let out a panicked yelp and leapt from CR-8R's head to hide behind Milo, who was still giggling. Meanwhile, CR-8R crashed into the holo-table and rolled across the floor before finally coming to a stop on his side.

"What are you doing?" Lina said, her hands on her hips.

"Just having a little fun," Milo said.

"Fun?" CR-8R exclaimed, turning himself upright. "That fleabag almost ripped out my audio-receptors."

"Well, you *did* say you couldn't stand the sound of Morq's voice!" Milo responded, the monkey-lizard peeking guiltily over his shoulder. "He was just putting his fingers in your ears for you!"

Lina couldn't believe this. She had honestly believed that something was wrong with the ship. Instead, it had all just been another argument between their droid and Milo's pet!

"We don't have time for this," she insisted. "We're about to start descending into Lothal's atmosphere. Crater needs to transmit a fake ID so the Imperials don't realize we're the *Whisper Bird*."

"I remember when I used to tell you what to do," CR-8R snapped, hovering away from the holo-table.

"She just likes to think she's in charge," Milo commented as he tickled Morq under the chin.

"Well, someone has to be the responsible one around here," Lina snapped at her brother. "Why don't you make yourself useful and be quiet!"

She stalked back to the cockpit, knowing full well that Milo and Morq would be sticking out their tongues at her back.

She didn't care. At least CR-8R was already in position, connecting to the *Bird*'s computer. Ahead of them, an Imperial freighter orbited Lothal, but CR-8R's supply of false identities would fool the Imperials into giving them permission to land.

Hopefully.

Thankfully, the false ID worked and the *Whisper Bird* was soon swooping down through Lothal's bright blue sky.

Milo and Morq had joined them in the cockpit. The earlier argument was already forgotten at the sight that lay ahead.

A city of gleaming towers sat on the horizon. Each skyscraper rose majestically from the ground like a glistening needle.

"That's where we're heading?" Milo asked.

"Capital City," Lina confirmed.

"It's beautiful," Milo said. "But what is *that* supposed to be?"

He pointed past the skyscrapers to a partially constructed black dome. Large cranes supported the structure as a cluster of chimneys spewed thick smoke into the atmosphere.

"The new Imperial base," CR-8R reported. "Lothal invited the Empire here three months ago. According to the local news channel, Lothal is to be the center of a new hyperspace route, providing safe passage across the galaxy."

Milo looked at the vast tracts of farmland below them. Massive automated machines were ripping up the crops, clearing kilometers and kilometers of wheat.

"Looks like the Empire wants more than a hyper-way," Milo noted.

"Lothal is rich in minerals," CR-8R reported. "I would think those farms are being cleared for mining."

Lina frowned. The Imperial dome looked menacing, looming up behind the graceful spires of Capital City. It didn't belong.

"Is that where we're heading?" Milo asked, indicating a busy spaceport to the right of the city.

Lina shook her head. "I wish. I've booked us into a cheap landing strip on the other side of the city. It'll be a bit of a walk."

Milo sighed. "Because we want to keep a low profile?"

"No, because we're running low on credits," Lina explained. "Capital City is an expensive place to visit."

"We may have another problem," CR-8R interjected.

"Which is?" Lina asked. She didn't want to hear any more bad news.

The droid tapped a gauge on the dashboard. "We're running dangerously low on fuel. If we don't replenish the fuel cells soon, we may not be able to even take off again."

"Let's worry about one thing at a time," Lina said. "I can see the landing strip."

Milo followed his sister's gaze out the cockpit windows.

"That's it?" he asked. The *Whisper Bird* had

swept around the skyscrapers and was heading
for a clump of squat, rundown buildings a
kilometer or so from Capital City. In the middle
of the shantytown lay a narrow strip of brown
earth dotted with decrepit ships.

"It's all we can afford," Lina reminded him.
"I'm taking us down."

With Lina at the controls, the *Whisper Bird*
touched down perfectly. Soft clay bubbled
around the landing pads.

"And you're sure the ship's not just going to sink into the ground?" Milo said as they carefully walked down the *Bird*'s ramp.

"I'm not sure of anything anymore," Lina admitted. She glanced around at their surroundings. Aliens were everywhere, milling around the ships or lounging outside the rickety buildings. Lina felt like everyone's eyes were on them.

"I suggest we keep moving," CR-8R piped up. "Some of these characters look rather unsavory. I think I'd rather spend more time with Morq than hang around here!"

They made their way across the muddy landing strip and headed for a road that led toward Capital City.

"What about the transmission?" Milo asked the droid. "Can you track it?"

CR-8R cocked his head as they passed the first building. "I can't even detect it anymore. Our mysterious rebel seems to have stopped broad—"

The droid stopped mid-word as a huge creature stepped in front of them. It was almost twice the size of Lina. It was a walking wall of muscle, with scaly skin and a cluster of tiny eyes beneath a solitary brow. Drool flowed uninhibited from its wide lipless mouth.

"Nice ship," the giant growled deeply. It's voice sounded as if it could easily shake planets apart.

"T-thanks," Lina stammered, grabbing Milo's arm. She tried to maneuver her brother around the nonhuman. "We like it."

The hulking alien blocked their way. "I like, too. I take it."

"It's not for sale," CR-8R informed him. The alien grinned, revealing rows of yellow teeth.

"Sell? You give to me!" the alien demanded.

"Is that right?" came an accented voice from behind them. The children turned to see another alien glaring at the giant with hooded bloodred eyes. This alien was tall. His powerful

frame was draped in a long, heavy cape with a large hood that rested on top of the two pointed horns on his head.

The larger bully backed away instantly.

"S-sorry," it stuttered, its multiple eyes wide with panic. "My mistake. Thought you someone else."

The giant turned and fled, faster than Lina would have thought possible.

"T-thanks," Lina said, looking at the newcomer skeptically.

"Not a problem," he replied. "This is not a safe place for children. You should come with me."

CR-8R put a mechanical hand on Lina's shoulder defensively. "Thank you for the kind offer, but I am sure we will be just fine on our own," he said.

The droid started guiding Milo and Lina away.

"Of course," the horned alien said, waving good-bye. "After all, it's not like you need help finding your transmission."

Milo turned back to the alien, who was grinning like a Danorian wolf. "How do you know we're even looking for one?"

The alien pulled down his hood to reveal two pointed ears, each furnished with gold rings.

"I couldn't help but overhear, kid," he grumbled. "The question is whether you're going to trust me or not?"

Lina took a hesitant step forward. "You can take us to the person who's making the transmissions?"

The alien's smirk grew wider. "Not personally, but I know someone who can help. For the right price, of course."

"And how much is that?" Lina said, trying to keep the trembling out of her voice.

The alien poked the tip of a pink tongue through sharp teeth. "That's something you'll need to ask my boss."

"Your boss?" CR-8R repeated. "We don't even know who you are, sir!"

"My apologies. How rude of me." The alien gave a mock bow. "Cikatro Vizago at your service."

CHAPTER 3
CRATE EXPECTATIONS

"ARE YOU SURE this is a good idea?" Milo asked as they flew along the road to Capital City.

"No," Lina replied. After introducing himself, Vizago had crammed the children and CR-8R onto the back of a landspeeder, which was now whizzing away from the landing strip. "But what choice did we have?"

"We could have gone back in the ship and flown away," CR-8R replied. "If we hadn't wasted all our fuel getting here in the first place."

"It won't be a waste if it can help us find Mom and Dad," Lina scolded him.

Vizago looked curiously over his shoulder. "Who's that you're trying to find?"

"It doesn't matter," Lina said quickly. She did not want to reveal too many secrets to the horned stranger. "We just need to find out who's behind those transmissions."

Vizago laughed. "That's what everyone wants to know. Especially the Imperials. Old Azadi is running out of time."

"Who?" Milo asked, shifting closer to the pilot.

"Him!" Vizago said, pointing to a large holo-screen on the side of a skyscraper. The face of a stern man glared back at them. "Ryder Azadi, governor of Lothal. The Empire's given him a month to find and capture whoever's been making those broadcasts."

"But you said your boss can find them."

"My boss can find anything."

"Then why doesn't he just tell the Empire?"

Vizago threw back his head and laughed. "My boss working with the Empire? That'll be the day. He'd be happier if they left and were never seen again." Vizago's smile faltered for a second. "Although I wouldn't hold your breath on that happening."

The landspeeder turned a corner. They were in the middle of the city now, the buildings stretching high into the air above them. All around people went about their business—speeder bikes dodging each other along the roads.

Everything looked so clean and new. It looked nothing like the slum they'd just come from.

And every now and then, between the towers, Milo caught a glimpse of the looming Imperial building that was being built on the other side of town.

"If no one likes them, why did Lothal invite the Empire here in the first place?" he asked.

"We didn't have a choice," Vizago replied. "Capital City may look wealthy, but the planet was broke. Lothal used to sell crops all over the galaxy, but ever since the Clone Wars, people on other planets can't afford to import food anymore. All of Lothal's customers started growing their own crops. With no money coming in, the planet was quickly in financial trouble."

"And that's when the Empire came knocking," Lina said quietly.

Vizago nodded. "We welcomed them with open arms. They had the solution to *all* our problems."

Milo and Lina could tell from Vizago's tone that he didn't believe a word of what he was saying. "Now they're here, there's no getting rid of them. But hey, Imperial credits are as good as everybody else's. The boss doesn't really mind, as long as the cash keeps coming in."

"You still haven't said what your boss does," Lina pointed out.

"You're right, I haven't," Vizago replied, slowing the landspeeder. "You can ask him yourself."

"Why are we stopping here?" Milo asked as they came to a halt beside a large warehouse.

"Because it's the end of the road."

Vizago jumped out of the speeder. He pointed proudly at a large sign that ran along the side of the building.

"'Twin Horns Storage,'" he read aloud. "My own little empire."

"You own a storage company?" Lina asked, hopping out after him.

"Yes and no," Vizago said. "Come on."

The alien marched toward the large front door.

"Can we trust him?" Milo whispered to his sister as they followed. Morq clutched tightly to Milo's neck.

"No!" CR-8R insisted. Lina just shrugged.

"Your guess is as good as mine, but we don't exactly have anyone else to ask."

Vizago stopped by the door and waited for them. "This way please, although the rat will have to stay."

Milo crossed his arms across his chest. "What rat?"

"That *thing*," Vizago said, pointing at Morq. "The boss is allergic to monkey-lizards. He uses them for target practice."

Morq squealed in alarm, clinging even tighter to Milo.

"You better wait here," Milo said, trying to free himself from the monkey-lizard's grip. "We won't be long, I promise."

"Allow me," CR-8R piped up, swinging one of his manipulator arms toward the animal. Morq snarled and jumped off Milo. He landed on the wall of the building and scampered up to the roof.

"That's better," Vizago said, leading them through the door. They found themselves in a large reception area, where a pair of golden droids sat behind the front desk. Vizago swaggered toward them.

"I've got some friends here to meet the boss."

The first droid shook its head, letting out a series of electronic chirps and whistles.

"I don't care if he's not available," Vizago snapped. "He'll want to see these guys, okay?"

The droid continued to argue, but Vizago wasn't having any of it. "Listen. Either you let me show my friends through, or I test my new blaster on your head."

To make his point, Vizago dropped his hand to the holster on his hip. The two droids whistled at each other before a door opened behind them.

"Thank you," Vizago sneered as he stalked past them.

"I thought you said you owned this place," Milo pointed out, chasing after the alien. "Shouldn't those two just do what you say?"

Vizago stopped at the doorway. "Don't ask too many questions, kid. Now, step through the archway."

Milo did what he was told. A red light washed over him as he passed through. Vizago checked a screen that was set into the wall.

"You're clear. You're not carrying any weapons. Now your turn, girlie."

He pointed at Lina, who stepped up beside her brother. The red light flashed, although this time it was accompanied by a warning bleep. Vizago frowned.

"Hands up."

"What for?" Lina asked, although she did as she was told. Vizago stalked over to her and grabbed her belt. Flipping open her belt pouch, he extracted one of the tools inside.

"What's this?" he asked, flicking the tool's

activation toggle. A tiny energy blade appeared at the tip.

"That's just my fusion torch."

Vizago regarded her with suspicion. "Why do you need a cutting tool?"

Milo jumped to his sister's defense. "You've never traveled in our ship. Lina's always having to fix things."

Vizago looked Lina up and down, sizing her up. "Little engineer, eh?"

"I try," she said, sticking out her chin.

He pushed the torch back into her hands.

"Just keep it in your belt, okay?" he said. He walked back to the controls before turning to CR-8R. "You're next, droid."

CR-8R hesitated. "I can assure you I have nothing to hide."

Vizago raised a heavy eyebrow. "You either do the scan, or I dismantle you piece by piece. . . ."

Grumbling, Crater hovered through the archway. "Oh, very well."

Vizago grinned as the screen bleeped again. "Perfect," he said, reading the results of the scan. "Absolutely perfect."

"Don't tell him that," Milo muttered under his breath. "His head is big enough as it is!"

"I heard that, Master Milo," CR-8R complained.

"I think you were supposed to," Vizago said, winking at Milo. "Come on."

He led them into a large chamber full of stacked crates, each the size of a landspeeder. The stacks stretched all the way up to the ceiling. Every crate looked exactly the same, with gray metal sides and no markings.

"Impressed?" Vizago asked, noting their open mouths.

"There's so many," Lina said. "There must be hundreds and hundreds."

"What's in them?" Milo asked.

Vizago tapped the side of his nose. "That's for me to know and you to never find out."

He stepped over to the arch and flipped a switch. A shutter slid down, sealing them in.

Beside Lina, CR-8R made an irritated tutting noise. "Are we supposed to be intimidated, sir?" the droid blurted out. "You're not fooling anyone."

Vizago regarded the droid with an amused expression. "Is that so?"

"That security arch is military grade, far too sophisticated for a second-rate storage company," CR-8R snapped.

"Oh, my company is second-rate now, is it?"

"No," the droid continued, ignoring Lina's attempts to shut him up. "You're worse than that. You're a crook. This entire 'business' is an obvious front for some kind of criminal enterprise."

Vizago's smile faded. "And how exactly would you know that?"

The droid wagged a mechanical finger at the alien. "Your company is as fake as you are,

Cikatro Vizago. I just checked the Galactic register. According to the tax records, Twin Horns Storage made little to no profit on the books last year. You want to know what's in the boxes, Master Milo? Nothing but weapons and stolen property, I'd bet. This is a smuggling den!"

"And this is Vilmarh's Revenge," Vizago snapped, a blaster suddenly in his hand. He was pointing it straight at the droid. "It was a gift from the boss. It's an antique, but a powerful one. Keep your vocalizer shut, or I'll blast the head from your shoulders—understand?"

"You can't do this," Lina said, putting herself between Vizago and the droid.

"Why can't I?" the horned alien sneered. "So I don't *exactly* operate within the law, but guess what? Neither does your mysterious broadcaster. And what about two kids and a droid on the run from the Empire? What does that make them?"

"How do you know the Empire's looking for us?"

Vizago's sneer returned. "I didn't—until now. Either way, I wouldn't be too picky about the company you keep."

With his point made, Vizago slipped his blaster back into its holster and walked over to a control console.

"So I don't know what's in all the boxes," he admitted, flipping open a panel to reveal a keypad. "That's the boss's business, but I do know that each crate has its own code. Just punch it in here . . ."

He tapped a five-digit code with one of his razor-sharp nails. Above them, one of the crates slid smoothly out of its stack.

"It's got repulsors!" Lina exclaimed.

"They all do," Vizago said as the crate descended toward them. "Enter the code and you get your box. Cool, huh?"

The large crate landed softly beside them, its repulsors humming.

Vizago grinned before calling out into the warehouse. "Hey, Rom, you there?"

His question was answered by footsteps as a green-skinned alien appeared from behind the nearest stack. This one was a Rodian with large round eyes and a prominent snout. As he approached, the alien pulled out a stubby blaster that he aimed straight at the children.

"Don't mind Rom," Vizago said. "He's just here to keep the contents of this box nice and safe."

"Safe," Rom repeated sluggishly.

"What's in it?" Milo asked.

"Nothing yet," replied Vizago as he slid open the crate's door to reveal an empty space inside. "Get in, now!"

CHAPTER 4
RASK ODAI

"YOU WANT US to get in there?" Lina asked, staring into the empty crate.

Vizago chuckled and turned to the Rodian. "She's a clever one, isn't she, Rom?"

The snout-nosed alien echoed Vizago's laugh. "Yeah, smart!"

"And what if we say no?" Milo asked.

Now Vizago's weapon was back in his palm. "We're the ones with the blasters, kid! What do you think will happen?"

Milo was fed up with being threatened. Looking behind Vizago and Rom, he shouted one word—"Morq!"

The two aliens turned slightly, expecting to see the monkey-lizard behind them, but it was the distraction that Milo needed. He darted around the empty crate and ran into the stacks. He had no idea where he was going, or what he would find. Maybe there was another exit. If he could get out of the warehouse, he could go find help.

Milo dashed around a nearby stack only to find himself looking at another pile of crates. He turned right and then left. There were just more crates everywhere, stacked all the way up to the ceiling. It was like being in a maze.

He picked a direction and ran in a straight line, passing column after column of boxes. Then, without warning, a crate slipped out of its stack in front of him. Milo skidded but couldn't help banging into its side. The clang of the impact echoed around the warehouse.

He ran back the way he'd come only to find another crate sliding across his path. More crates were hovering into place, boxing Milo in.

Vizago must be operating them remotely, Milo thought. He jumped up, trying to climb the sides of the box in front of him, but the smooth metal was too slippery. He was trapped! There was nowhere to go.

"Not bad," Vizago called from above. Milo looked up to see the alien standing on top of a floating crate. "You've got spirit. The boss will like that."

"Didn't get me very far," Milo grumbled, glaring up at his captor.

"Don't beat yourself up, kid," Vizago said with a grin. "We're professionals."

Vizago marched Milo back to his sister and CR-8R. Lina threw her arms around him tightly. "What were you thinking, Milo? They could have blasted you!"

He knew it was stupid, but he'd needed to try, although it hadn't done them any good. Rom herded them all into the crate. He followed them through the open door with his blaster trained on them. Milo covered his nose. The inside of the crate reeked of rotten fish.

"Enjoy your trip," Vizago called from the outside.

"Wait!" Lina pleaded. "What are you going to do with us?"

Smirking, Vizago pressed a button on the side of the box and the door slid shut, plunging them into darkness. Milo ran forward and banged on the closed door.

"Let us out of here! Let us out!"

Lights flickered to life on the ceiling, illuminating the claustrophobic box.

"Away from the door," Rom grunted as the crate lurched. The repulsors powered up with a whine.

Outside, they could hear the keypad beep as Vizago entered a longer, eight-digit code.

"We're moving," CR-8R said, lunging forward to catch Milo, who stumbled with the sudden movement.

Milo steadied himself. It felt like they were flying into the air.

"You can't keep us in here," Lina told Rom. "We have friends who know we're here," she lied. "Big friends. With bigger blasters than yours."

"I like blasters," Rom said blankly.

Lina joined her brother and the droid.

"Crater," she whispered. "Can you burn your way out of this?"

CR-8R turned to look at the walls of the crate. "I don't know. That looks like duramentium, one of the toughest steels in the galaxy."

Lina sighed. "Which means my fusion torch will be next to useless, too."

CR-8R nodded. "Unfortunately, that warty thug would blast us before we could even make a dent."

"Rom blasts fast," the Rodian commented. Milo sighed. There was obviously nothing wrong with Rom's ears.

The box shifted beneath their feet, changing direction.

Lina turned to the Rodian. "Where are you taking us?"

"Yeah," Milo said. "And why did Vizago trap you in here, too?"

Rom didn't answer.

"Can you understand me?" Milo said, speaking louder and slower. "Why. Are. You. Here?"

"Rom not trapped," the alien replied. "You not trapped, either."

"Well, it certainly looks that way to me," CR-8R commented before a sudden jolt caused him to dip slightly on his repulsors. Milo fell back into Lina, who slipped her hand into his. They'd stopped moving.

"Now what?" Lina asked.

"Now you meet boss," Rom informed her as the door slid open to reveal a long narrow room beyond. Without another word, the Rodian stepped out of the crate and onto thick carpet.

"I assume we're supposed to follow," CR-8R said, and they did exactly that.

The room had been constructed from four or five crates bolted together. It had the same lights in the ceiling, although the smooth walls were lined with exotic works of art. There were paintings of seascapes and underwater worlds. At the far end was a beautifully carved desk with a high-backed chair. Above the desk, half a dozen hovering platforms buzzed in the air like insects. Each held treasures of a bygone age. There were giant crystals, an ornate metal box, and an armored gauntlet. However, Milo's eyes were fixed on the hulking figure that stood behind the desk.

"Oh, my," CR-8R said, his synthetic voice quivering. "An IG assassin droid."

"Yes, Crater," Lina said, trying to shut him up.

"You don't understand, Miss Lina," CR-8R continued regardless. "Assassin droids are incredibly dangerous. They're walking armories, complete with integrated concussion grenade launchers and flamethrowers."

"Yes, Crater. Enough now."

"Although I've always been quite jealous of their acid-proof servo wires. I've always wanted some of th—"

"Crater, shut up!" Lina snapped.

"Droid talks a lot," Rom said, stopping beside the table.

"Tell us something we don't know," Milo replied before turning his attention to the assassin droid. "Are you the boss?"

"No, he is not!" came a voice from hidden speakers. Milo looked around to see where it was coming from. "Who said that?"

"Is IG-70 the boss? Ha!" the voice continued as a panel opened in one of the walls. Milo gasped. Beyond the wall a tank of yellow, briny water was being held back by a force field. Swimming in the murky liquid was an imposing figure with large bulbous eyes on the sides of a high-domed head. Milo immediately recognized the alien as a native of Mon Cala. The *Whisper Bird* had visited the watery planet when Milo was little. Their father had made many friends among the Mon Calamari when he'd first started exploring the Outer Rim. But this one did not look friendly.

"Boss," Rom chimed in helpfully as the alien swam through the energy barrier that kept the water from flooding the room. Dripping all over the expensive carpet, the Mon Calamari

slopped over to the desk to sit down with a squelch on the chair.

"Boss have good bath?" Rom asked.

"No, I did not," the alien snapped. "The water's stale. Recycle it, will you?"

Rom did what he was told, pressing a control beside the tank. Behind the force field, the murky liquid drained away and was replaced with much cleaner water.

"Now," the Mon Calamari said, sniffing the air. "Who are you? And why do you smell of monkey-lizards?"

"Who are we?" Milo repeated, sounding braver than he felt. "The better question is who are *you*?"

The alien's nostrils flared and he turned to Rom. "This is why I don't like children," he gurgled. "Impertinent sea slugs."

"Sea slugs," Rom repeated, sounding like he hadn't understood a word that his boss had just said.

The Mon Calamari leaned forward as water pooled around his elbows. "I am Rask Odai, and this is my planet."

"I thought it was the Empire's planet," Lina pointed out.

"That's what I let them believe." He waved a webbed hand dismissively. "Oh, they can worry about *governing*, and *law* and *order*. That's all too boring for me. I'm more interested in the important things in life." He grinned, revealing toothless gums. "Like money!"

All the time, Odai's goggle-like eyes were focused on CR-8R. Milo watched as the Mon Calamari licked his blubbery lips. Milo shuddered. Did this fishy freak eat droids or something?

Odai's watery eyes were still locked on the droid. "What do you want?" he said.

"Didn't Vizago let you know why we're here?" Lina asked.

"If he did, I wouldn't have to ask!" Odai snapped, his voice rising.

"S-sorry," Lina said, raising her hands apologetically. Slowly, she told the gangster why they'd come to Lothal and how they were looking for the source of the rebel transmissions.

"Is that all?" Odai replied, scratching the long fronds that dangled from his bottom lip. "That's easy."

"Easy," Rom repeated.

Odai opened a drawer in his desk and pulled out a handheld device.

"I don't suppose either of you understand communication frequencies?" the crime lord gurgled.

"Lina does," Milo said. "She's great with machines."

"Is she now?" Odai said. He beckoned her over with a webbed finger.

Lina cautiously stepped closer under the ever-watchful gaze of the assassin droid.

Odai started working the scanner, and static burst out of the speakers. Lina walked around the table to see what the Mon Calamari was doing. With the twist of a dial, a voice broke through the static—cultured and cold.

"*All troops report to barracks. Training will commence at—*"

Odai turned another control and the voice dissolved again. "We use these to eavesdrop on our Imperial neighbors," he explained. "Just in case they're doing anything . . . interesting. Now, if you take a scanner like this and use it to search for background chatter, channels that only droids use for communication . . ."

Another voice broke through, but it wasn't an Imperial message this time.

"*We'll be back on the airwaves later today. In the meantime, stand up for what you believe, not what the Emperor tells you to think. You were born free. Hold on to that. Treasure it.*"

"That's it," Milo said, excitedly. "That's the transmission!"

Odai pressed a couple of buttons, showing Lina each step of the process. "Get the scanner to lock onto the signal and you should be able to track it, see? Like a detector." The device started to beep rhythmically. "The closer you get to the source of the broadcast, the louder the beep."

"That's amazing," Lina admitted.

Odai slammed the scanner down onto the top of the table. "I know. Now, about my payment . . ."

"Payment?" she said, glancing nervously at Milo. "Vizago never said anything about payment."

"What do you think I am, a charity?" Odai sneered. "I gave you what you want, now you have to give me something."

"But we don't have any money," Milo tried to argue. "Not much anyway."

"I don't want your credits," Odai snapped.

"Then what do you want?" Lina asked.

Odai turned to the assassin droid. "IG-70?"

The droid nodded. "Understood."

With that, the tall droid marched from the back of the room, heading straight for Milo and CR-8R.

"What's he going to do?" Lina asked the Mon Calamari.

"Collect my payment," Odai replied, rubbing his webbed fingers together.

"Keep back," CR-8R warned, putting himself in front of Milo. "I won't let you hurt these children."

"Understood," IG-70 repeated as he reached up and grabbed CR-8R's metal face.

With an electronic grunt, the assassin droid ripped CR-8R's head clean from his shoulders!

CHAPTER 5
THE *MOVEABLE FEAST*

"WHAT ARE YOU DOING?" Milo cried as sparks burst from CR-8R's neck. The headless droid's arms dropped lifelessly to his sides as IG-70 marched his prize back toward Odai.

Milo sprung forward, trying to grab CR-8R's head, but the giant assassin droid swatted him aside.

"Give it to me," Odai gurgled, his arms outstretched. He snatched CR-8R's head from IG-70 and turned it over in his fingers. "Yes, yes. This is perfect. Absolutely perfect."

"Give that back," Lina said, lunging for the head only to find IG-70's blaster pointing directly at her.

"You will freeze," the droid rumbled.

Lina unwillingly raised her hands and took a step back.

"But what do you want with Crater's head?" Milo asked from the floor.

"You're kidding, right?" the Mon Calamari said, his pink tongue wetting those horribly blubbery lips. "This is a genuine architect droid head. A Mark IV. I haven't seen one for decades."

"So what if it is?" asked Lina. "It belongs to CR-8R, not you!"

"It's payment for the services I provided," Odai snapped back. "You have your transmission. I have the droid's head. Fair and square."

"But it can't be worth anything to you!"

"Not worth anything? This will be the jewel in my collection." He threw out his other arm and indicated the treasures on the floating platforms.

"Among that junk?" Milo shouted.

"Junk? This isn't junk!" Odai scoffed. "I have the finest collection of Old Republic artifacts this side of Nar Shaddaa. This head was wasted on your droid. It's an antique."

He opened another drawer in his desk and pulled out a hover-platform. Setting CR-8R's head on a stand, Odai gurgled with pleasure as it floated out of his hands to join the rest of his collection.

"No!" Milo cried, jumping up toward the desk. "You can't just go around stealing people's heads!"

An arm snaked around his neck, pulling him back as a blaster pressed hard against his head. It was Rom. The Rodian hissed in Milo's ear.

"Boss can do anything he wants."

"Besides," Odai added, admiring his latest acquisition, "I didn't steal anything. It was a legitimate trade. Now get these two sea slugs out of my sight!"

On the streets of Lothal, a figure in a long cloak swept back and forth on a speeder bike.

As he scanned the streets, the comlink on his wrist buzzed. The man raised the device to his hooded face.

"Have you found them?" someone asked over the comms-signal.

"Not yet," he replied. "Are we sure they're even here?"

Before his contact could reply, a landspeeder roared up along the road. The man backed his bike into an alleyway to observe the craft slow to a stop.

It was piloted by a Devaronian, who was flanked by a Rodian and an old assassin droid. As the man watched, the two aliens threw a boy and a girl from the back of the speeder. The children landed in a pile in the dirt as the Rodian tossed a heap of broken machinery from the floating vehicle behind them. It was a droid without a head. It bobbed along lifelessly on its repulsors.

"Please don't do this!" the girl said.

"How are you going to stop us?" The
Devaronian laughed. "Now do yourself a favor,
kid, and don't come back!"

With that, the three rogues zoomed off,
leaving the children lying in the road.

The man spoke into his comlink. "Do you see
them?"

"Yes," came the reply.

"Shall I bring them in?"

"Not yet," his contact told him. *"We need to be sure. . . ."*

It was a long walk back to the landing strip. By the time they'd reached the shantytown, Milo and Lina's feet were aching and their hearts were heavy. They had started the journey by talking about what they would do to Rask Odai when they saw him again, imagining all kinds of revenge. But the reality was that it was hopeless.

"Even if we could get past the security arch, we'd never be able to find his office again, not without knowing the code to enter into the crate controls," Lina said, pulling CR-8R's floating body behind her.

"And then there's Rom and that assassin droid," Milo added. "You think they'll just let us take Crater's head?"

The *Whisper Bird* was in front of them as they trudged across the muddy port. "We'll think of something," Lina promised him. "There'll

be something on board the *Bird* that can help.
You'll see!"

But Milo's eyes had gone wide. "Morq! I
forgot about Morq!" He looked around, panicked
by the sudden realization. "He must still be back
at Twin Horns Storage!"

"Maybe he came back to the *Bird*?" Lina
suggested, but Milo was already racing for the
ship, slipping in the mud. He ran around the
Whisper Bird, calling the monkey-lizard's name.

His voice was becoming increasingly frantic with every shout.

"Morq! *Morq!*"

Leaving CR-8R's body behind, Lina ran up to him. "Milo, keep it down. People are looking!"

"He's not here, Lina," Milo said. "He's back in the city. He's probably so scared and he's all alone."

And with that Milo's face crumpled as tears started to flow. Lina couldn't move fast enough to stop her brother from collapsing to his knees in the mud. He rested his face in his hands.

She dropped down beside him, throwing her arms around him. She pulled him close.

"There, there," she said, her own voice catching as she realized that it was usually their mom who said those words. "It's going to be okay."

"No, it's not," he cried out as sobs shook his body. "Morq's gone. Crater's gone. Mom and Dad are gone. And there's nothing we can do about it."

"Of course there is," Lina told him, although she wasn't sure she believed it herself. There they were in the shadow of the *Whisper Bird* on a strange planet with no friends. The tears that ran down her own face were long overdue. Both of them had gone through so much, and they were still no nearer finding their parents. It seemed like the entire galaxy was against them. If it wasn't the Empire, it was evil creatures, and if it wasn't evil creatures, it was gangsters like Odai.

As she sat cradling her brother, Lina had finally run out of ideas. Sure there were the transmissions. But even if what Odai had told them was true, how did they know they could trust whoever was making the broadcasts? How could they trust anyone anymore?

"Looks like someone needs a good lunch!" someone called out.

Lina looked up, her arms still around Milo. A woman was standing in front of them, her hands on her hips. She had a kind, open face,

with dark skin and bright green eyes. Her hair
was bunched into tight curls, held in place with
a bright orange band. She wore a long knitted
shawl over an apron and a pair of faded overalls.

"Unless you're not hungry," she added when
neither of them replied.

"I am," Milo said meekly, wiping the back of
his hand across his nose.

Lina smiled. Even when he was upset, Milo
always thought with his stomach. "It *has* been a
while since we ate anything."

"Then what are you waiting for?" the woman said. "Follow me."

Nervously, Milo got to his feet, wiping tears away with his sleeve. Together, they walked hand in hand, following the woman around the *Whisper Bird*.

Parked in the next bay was another ship that hadn't been there before. It was a very old freighter—the kind Lina's mom had shown her in old holo-reels. It looked like it had seen a lot of action. Its dented hull was pitted with years of asteroid strikes. That wasn't the strangest thing about it though. One of the cargo doors was open, revealing what looked like a small kitchen and counter. Metal tables were dotted around the opening, each occupied by the aliens who had watched the children's arrival with suspicion. Now they were stuffing their faces with hot meals. Taking a deep breath, Lina smelled soups, stews, and freshly baked bread. Her stomach gurgled. She was hungry, too. She hadn't realized how hungry until that moment.

"Come on in," the woman said, beckoning them forward. "Welcome to the *Moveable Feast*. Yes, there are prettier ships out there, faster ships even, but none that serve food like Captain Shalla Mondatha's. Here, take a seat."

She pulled out a stool from a free table, producing a cloth from her pocket to wipe the metal surface clean.

"Captain who?" Milo asked, slipping onto the stool.

"Shalla Mondatha," the woman repeated. "You must have heard the name?"

"I'm afraid not," Lina admitted, sitting next to her brother.

"Well, you have now," the woman said, beaming. "You're looking at her. I'm the captain, cook, and dishwasher. It's a pleasure to meet you."

Suddenly, there was a clashing of plates. Lina turned to see a chubby Dowutin trying to stop a small scavenger from eating his lunch. In trying to swat the creature away, the orange-skinned alien had knocked over his table.

"Hey!" Shalla shouted. "Watch what you're doing!"

"It's this thing," the Dowutin complained, pointing behind the overturned table. "It was stealing my food."

There was an angry squeak, and Milo jumped up from his stool. "Wait! That's—"

At the sound of Milo's voice, Morq jumped onto the overturned table. The monkey-lizard let out a squeal of joy and raced over to hop into Milo's arms. Lina's brother hugged his pet, who licked Milo's face happily.

"Someone's excited to see you," Shalla said with a laugh.

"Morq! I thought I'd lost you! But you came back! Of course you did, you clever boy!"

"What about my food?" the Dowutin complained.

"By the size of that belly, it looks like you've had enough," Shalla shouted back. "Move along. I've got hungry mouths to feed."

Turning her attention back to the children,

Shalla pulled a datapad from her apron pocket. "Now what can I get for you. Today's specials are Melahnese red curry, Melahnese green curry, and Melahnese yellow curry."

"Do you have anything that isn't Melahnese curry?" Milo asked.

"Of course I do." Shalla laughed, her eyes sparkling. "I can make you nerf pie, berbersian crab salad, bhudde and orxtle stew . . ."

"Nerf pie please," Milo said, his earlier tears forgotten.

Shalla smiled and turned to Lina. "And for you, dear?"

"The salad, please."

"Do you want dindra sauce with that?"

Lina licked her lips. She hadn't tasted dindra in years.

"Yes, please!"

Shalla gave the children another dazzling smile and slipped the datapad back into her apron pocket. "You got it!"

She disappeared into the *Feast*. She

reappeared a few minutes later with two plates stacked high with food.

Milo gazed at the giant slab of pie as it was placed in front of him. "That looks amazing!"

Lina's salad looked just as inviting. "It does, but how much will it cost?" She looked up at the captain, biting her lip. "We don't have a lot of credits."

Shalla leaned close to them. "It's on the house," she whispered. "Just don't tell everyone. They'll all be wanting freebies!"

She pulled up a stool of her own and sat at the table. "What are you waiting for? Eat up!"

The children didn't need to be told twice. Grabbing cutlery from a metal tub, they dug into their meals, cramming forkfuls of the gorgeous food into their mouths. Everything tasted so good. The Naboo lettuce was crisp and fresh, while the buttered crab sticks melted on Lina's tongue. And the sauce was so tangy her taste buds felt like they were dancing!

"Good?" Shalla inquired.

"Moh yefph!" Milo said with his mouth full.

Shalla laughed. "You know, I travel this entire sector, setting up shop from port to port. I've cooked for freighter crews all along the Kessel Run. But I've never seen anyone enjoy my food as much as you two!"

"It's really good," Lina said, taking another bite.

Shalla smiled fondly. Then, for a moment a deep sadness seemed to shadow her usually cheerful features. "You remind me of my own daughter."

"Does she travel with you?" Milo asked.

"Heavens no," Shalla replied, regaining her composure. "She's all grown up now. Off having adventures of her own—but it's good to feed you two. Don't see a lot of kids in places like this, with good reason."

She placed a kind hand on Lina's arm. "What *are* you doing here, honey?"

Maybe it was the food in their bellies, or

the warmth of Shalla's smile, but the children told her everything. About their parents, about Captain Korda, about coming to Lothal and losing CR-8R's head.

"They just ripped it from his shoulders?" Shalla asked in amazement as they finished their story.

Suddenly, Lina felt the pang of loss again. "And we need it back. Crater's one of the most annoying droids you've ever met. He's stubborn and argumentative, but—"

"But he's yours," Shalla said softly.

Lina nodded. "He's all we've got left."

"Plus these maps your mom left you . . ." Shalla continued.

"Are in his head," Milo told Shalla.

"Well, that settles it," Shalla said. "First, I'm going to get you both a bowl of Bosphian trifle and then we're going to make plans."

Milo frowned, wiping a crumb from his lips. "Plans for what?"

Shalla smiled slyly. "Oh, I wasn't always a cook, Milo Graf. Long ago, in another life, I used to be a *smuggler*."

Lina's eyes widened.

"I've picked up a few tricks over the years," Shalla continued. "This Odai guy stole your droid's head? Well, we're going to steal it right back!"

CHAPTER 6
BEETLES

LATER THAT DAY, as Lothal's sun began
to sink in the sky, Shalla Mondatha zoomed
up to the entrance of Twin Horns Storage on
a shiny silver speeder bike. She still wore her
old knitted shawl, but the apron was gone and
a wrap-around visor covered her eyes. Behind
her speeder a medium-sized container bumped
along, hovering on a repulsor bed. She peered
through the open doors, watching Cikatro
Vizago's goons lugging crates around the lobby.
Her eyes narrowed behind her glasses as she
watched a Rodian slink down the street and
through the doors.

That must be Rom, she thought, recalling what the children had told her. Taking a deep breath, she steadied herself. It was now or never.

Leaping from the bike, she disconnected the crate and pushed it into the warehouse.

"Hey," Vizago said, stepping in front of her. "Where are you going with that?"

Shalla narrowed her eyes. "What do you mean?"

The Devaronian tapped her crate. "What I said! Where are you going with this container?"

Shalla shrugged. "It's supposed to go in my crate." She looked around, pretending ignorance. "This is Twin Corn Storage, isn't it?"

"Twin *Horns*," Vizago corrected her. "But this is a private business."

Shalla gave him a big smile. "Then I'm in the right place. I had my droid open an account earlier today. I need somewhere safe to store my ingredients when I'm off-world." When he didn't comment, Shalla added her name helpfully. "Captain Shalla Mondatha."

Vizago glanced at one of the two golden droids behind the main counter. It was already checking the Twin Horns's customer lists. Finding a name on the screen, the droid murmured a reply to Vizago.

The Devaronian turned back toward her, a

fake smile on his lips. "My mistake. I understand you paid for our premium service."

Shalla nodded enthusiastically. "Oh, yes. Only the best for my food."

"We're going to have to scan your crate,"Vizago said. "Nothing personal, you understand. Just standard procedure."

"Of course," Shalla replied. "That's why I chose your establishment. 'Security is our business,' isn't that what your brochure said?"

Vizago gave her another fake smile before turning to the Rodian. "Rom, scan the crate."

The Rodian looked confused. "But Rom see boss?"

"You can see him *after* you've scanned the crate," Vizago insisted.

Grumbling, Rom grabbed a handheld scanner and waved it over the container. Immediately, the scanner beeped furiously.

"Picked up life sign!" Rom reported.

Vizago's smile faded. "Open it."

Shalla shook her head. "I-I can't do that."

"Then it can't stay here," he snarled.

"You don't understand!"

"Then show me."

Shalla sighed, letting her shoulders drop. "Very well. It looks like I have no choice."

"No," Vizago agreed. "You don't."

Shalla ran her hand along the side of the container until she found a control. She pressed the button and the lid opened on its hinges, squeaking noisily.

A swarm of rainbow-colored beetles burst from the open container, spilling onto the floor. The Devaronian jumped back.

"Ugh! What are they?"

"Wakizan beetles," Shalla said, watching the insects scurry everywhere. "They're quite the delicacy in the Core worlds. I fry them in troogan oil." She fished a paper bag out of her pocket, offering it to the disgusted Devaronian. "Would you like to try one?"

"No, I wouldn't!" Vizago insisted as Shalla offered one to Rom instead. The Rodian took a beetle gladly, popping it into his snout and crunching loudly.

"Rom like!" he announced, and Shalla gave him another. Step one of the plan was in progress.

Step two happened as a red-furred creature scampered into the lobby, making a beeline for the beetles. It was Morq, chattering happily at the free meal.

"And now the monkey-runt is back," Vizago shouted. "Today just gets better. Shut the lid. Shut the lid!"

"Yes, of course," Shalla said, fiddling with the control. She pretended that it wasn't working. "Oh, I think it's stuck."

Meanwhile, Morq jumped around, scattering the insects everywhere.

"Can Rom see boss now?" Rom asked.

"Yes," Vizago snapped. "Go! There'll be one less pest here!"

Rom ran off. He hit the control pad on the security arch at the front of the warehouse with one of his sticky fingers. Shalla watched as a crate started floating toward Rom, presumably to take the Rodian to Odai.

Finally, she pressed the lid closed, cutting off the flow of beetles.

"I'm so sorry," Shalla said as an excited Morq leaped onto Vizago's head to swing off the alien's horns. "But if I didn't have to open the container . . ."

"Yes, yes," Vizago barked, trying to grab the monkey-lizard. Shalla used the distraction to look around the warehouse. Rom was gone now, but she was staring at the keypad he'd used. The hidden camera in her visor took a picture.

She pulled out a small metal tin and started to scatter tiny pellets on the floor. Morq jumped down and popped one into his mouth before spitting it back out in disgust. He darted back toward the street.

"Now what are you doing?" Vizago moaned.

"It's beetle food. They won't be able to resist, see?" Sure enough, the insects started scurrying toward her, following the trail of pellets. "I can't cook with them now, but I can get rid of them for you. Will you deliver my container into storage?"

"Yes, yes," Vizago grumbled. "If you clear my lobby, I'll deliver it any way you want."

Shalla grinned. "Thank you! I look forward to doing more business with you."

Before Vizago could cancel her account, Shalla hurried out of the building. The hungry beetles scuttled after her. When they were far enough away from the front doors, she threw the tin to the side, where it clattered against a wall. The food spilled everywhere, and the beetles descended on it.

The doors of Twin Horns Storage swung shut. Shalla returned to her speeder bike and found Morq waiting for her on the saddle. She gave the monkey-lizard a friendly tickle under the chin. "Good work, boy. That went better than I hoped."

She pressed a hidden button on the side of her visor and viewed the image she had taken of the keypad. "*Much* better."

With the press of another button, she transmitted the picture to a second pair of glasses inside the building. Nudging Morq out of the way, she threw her leg over the speeder bike and started the engine.

Their plan was in motion!

CHAPTER 7
FIRE ALARM

IN TWIN HORNS STORAGE, Cikatro
Vizago crushed a lone beetle under his boot.

"Bugs," he complained, lifting his foot. There
was a gloopy mess on the floor. "I hate them."

"What should we do with this thing?" said
one of his lackeys. He was a trunk-nosed
Onodone with a black patch over one of his
eyes.

Vizago looked at the container and sighed.
"She's paid her money, so we better look after it.
I've got a feeling that Captain Mondatha is the
kind of woman who would go to the authorities
if we lost her stock. But wait. . . ."

The Devaronian walked over to a side desk and pulled out two rods. He held them over the container and they jumped from his hands onto the lid.

"Gravity seals," he explained to the puzzled Onodone. "Just in case any of those insects try to push open the lid. Nothing can get out of it now."

Inside the container, someone desperately wanted to get out. Beneath the pile of squirming beetles, Lina and Milo were curled up in balls.

Both of them wore black jumpsuits and gloves that Shalla had provided. She'd promised that the beetles wouldn't be able to burrow in through the seams. Visor-like glasses protected their eyes, and breathing masks were clamped over their mouths.

Lina had her arms wrapped tightly around her head, her eyes screwed tight behind the

visor. This was the worst thing she'd ever had
to do. The beetles were everywhere! The bugs
were packed in so tightly that they could barely
move, but their little legs scratched against Lina
and Milo. And the noise of hundreds of tiny jaws
clicking together was horrifying!

She wanted to scream and brush the horrible

creatures away from her body but knew she couldn't.

The container was moving again, swaying as it was pushed deeper into the warehouse. She'd heard Vizago's muffled command through the constant chatter of the insects.

"Take it to the holding area for processing. We'll deal with it later."

Just as Shalla had predicted, Vizago and his crew would leave the container alone long enough for them to escape. Even so, Lina was starting to panic. What if the plan didn't work? What if Shalla's beetles were put straight into a storage crate? They'd be trapped until someone opened the box again. Or worse, they'd be left there, in the darkness, with the insects.

Lina forced herself to calm down. They'd worked it all out. Shalla had told them exactly what to do. Lina just had to be patient.

The container thudded as it was lowered to the floor, scaring the beetles. Lina listened until she heard the footsteps fade away.

Count to ten, she told herself, *maybe twenty. Make sure there's no one around.*

Everything was silent, except for the chattering of the insects. The container had been left in the processing area.

"Milo," she hissed through her breathing mask. "We need to move!"

Her brother shifted beside her, pushing up through the beetles to shove against the lid of the container.

"It won't budge . . ." he said, grunting with the effort. "Those gravity seals must be on too tight."

Lina shifted around, planting her feet against the side of the container. "Shalla said there's a loose panel over here, just in case something heavy got stacked on top."

She pushed against it with her feet. But nothing happened.

"It's stuck. Help me, will you?"

Milo joined her, pushing against the side with his own feet. Still nothing.

"Why isn't it moving?" Lina started to kick,

not caring if anyone heard her. She had to get out of there. Now.

"Lina, calm down," Milo urged. "We can do this. We just need to work together."

"No," she said, kicking the panel after every word. "Need. To. Get. Out. Now."

With the last kick, the loose panel came free and clattered on the floor. The beetles streamed out like a wave, Lina wriggling her way through the gap. As soon as she was out of the container, she jumped to her feet and brushed the last remaining beetles from her.

Milo slid out beside her. "Keep it down!"

She froze. He was right. Had anyone heard them?

As the beetles scampered to freedom, the children stood, listening. There were no shouts, no running footsteps.

They'd done it.

Pulling her breathing mask down, Lina ran to the corner of a stack of crates and peered around. They were alone in the warehouse, at least for now.

She glanced along the wall, spotting a red button behind protecting glass. It was an alarm, like the one by the arch. She nodded at Milo, who raced across to the wall, keeping his head down. Turning his face away, he smashed the glass and pressed the button. The alarm sounded immediately and an ear-splitting cry echoed around the warehouse. Milo ran back as they heard people headed toward the exit. Then they heard a whine from above as a crate descended. It landed in front of the security arch and the door slid open. Lina watched as Rask Odai exited the crate, flanked by Rom and IG-70 as they hurried their complaining boss out of the warehouse.

Lina waited for the main doors to close before grabbing Milo's arm and pulling him toward the crate. They reached the keypad and Lina pressed a button on the side of her visor. An image appeared on the back of the lens. It was the picture Shalla had taken using a special filter that highlighted Rom's oil-covered fingerprints on the buttons. If Lina worked back from the faintest print to the oiliest, she'd be able to figure out the code that would take them to Odai's office.

That was the theory anyway.

Milo was already in the crate. "Come on! Hurry, Lina!"

"I'm going as fast as I can," she said, following the fingerprints to type out the code. The keypad beeped as Lina completed the sequence. She jumped through the door just as it began to close.

Inside the crate, the lights flickered on, and they began to rise, the repulsors lifting them high into the air. The trip seemed to take even longer than their first one.

"Do you think they've figured out that there's no fire yet?" Lina asked.

"I hope not," Milo replied as the crate clanked into place.

The door slid open to reveal Odai's office, and the children ran toward the ornate desk.

"There it is!" Milo shouted, pointing at CR-8R's head floating on its platform.

"It's too high up!"

Milo grabbed Odai's chair and pulled it beneath the hovering shelf. "Hold this steady."

As he clambered onto the chair, the alarm stopped screeching.

"That's the end of the fire alarm," Milo said.

"Then they'll be coming back," Lina said frantically. "Hurry up!"

"Okay," Milo said, stretching up. It was still too high, and his fingers barely reached the bottom of the platform.

"Let me do it," Lina told him. "I'm taller."

"I can do it," Milo insisted, standing on tiptoe to grab the edge of the platform. Beneath him, the chair flipped over and he fell. He knocked

into the platform as he tumbled to the floor. CR-8R's head wobbled before falling over the edge and landing on Milo's back.

There was no time to celebrate. A new siren cut through the air, shriller than even the fire alarm.

"Warning!" a computerized voice boomed.

"Robbery in progress! Warning! Robbery in progress!"

Lina grabbed CR-8R's head and helped Milo to his feet. "I think we just lost the element of surprise!"

CHAPTER 8
FLUSHED

AT THE FAR END of the office, the children's crate dropped away. Lina ran to look down at the rapidly descending crate. "This is your fault. If you had just let me get Crater's head, we would never have set off the alarm."

Milo joined her at the edge of the room. "My fault? You were supposed to be holding the chair!" He peered at the warehouse floor far below. "We're a long way up, aren't we?"

"I guess Odai likes looking down at his kingdom."

"Yeah, speaking of Odai . . ." Milo said, pointing at another crate that was rising toward them. Its door was already open and the Mon

Calamari was standing in the gap. Rom and IG-70 were beside him, their blasters raised.

"They don't look happy to see us," Milo said as the first shots hammered against the outside of the office.

"What are we going to do?" Lina asked, jumping away from the opening. She looked around the office in desperation. "That's the only way out."

Milo's hand went to the breathing mask around his neck. "No, it's not. When did we last take a bath?"

Lina stared at the tank of water set into the wall. "You're joking!"

Milo ran back to the floating platforms and hopped onto the desk to grab a large silver box from one of the pedestals.

"That should do it," he said, jumping back down to the carpet.

"Do what?"

Milo opened the box's lid and ran back to Lina. "I don't know if CR-8R's head is waterproof."

"You're not joking," Lina groaned, slipping the droid's head inside the box. Milo snapped the lid shut.

"Nope. You first."

"Why me?"

The whine of the approaching crate was getting louder with every second.

"Okay, okay," Milo conceded. "I'll lead the way, if you're scared."

Lina shot him a withering look as he popped his breathing mask over his mouth and hurried to the force field. Taking a deep breath, he pushed his hand through the energy barrier. He quickly pulled his hand back out as soon as it got wet.

"It's freezing!"

"Changing your mind?"

An energy bolt shot through the open door to slam against the ceiling.

"Not on your life," Milo said, jumping through the force field. Lina ran to the controls and tried to remember how Rom had operated the flush.

"Stop where you are!" someone shouted from the open door. The crate was almost in place and IG-70's blaster was pointing right at her. "Drop the head!"

"No, don't!" Odai yelled. "You'll break it! Just stay where you are!"

"Sorry, can't do that," Lina shouted back. "See you later!"

She slammed her palm down on the control and the water whooshed from the tank, taking Milo with it. Clutching the metal box to her chest, Lina dived into the force field. She had the vague impression of two blaster bolts passing behind her before she plunged into the icy water.

It was like jumping into a whirlpool. One second she was in the tank and the next she was being sucked down a pipe, bashing against its slimy sides as she was pushed along by the current. She called out for Milo, but there was no answer. All she could do was hold on to the box and hope for the best.

Her head bumped against the side of the pipe, knocking her visor from her face. Salty water stung her eyes as she looked around, trying to see her brother.

She suddenly slammed into him—hard!

He cried out in pain as the remainder of the water washed past them, out through the circular grate that Milo had crashed into.

"Are you okay?" she asked, pulling her breathing mask aside.

Milo was pushing against the grill. "This thing won't budge."

She put the silver box to the side and joined in, heaving against the heavy metal grate. The stink coming from the other side told her that they were probably down in Lothal's sewer system, but as long as they were nowhere near Odai and his goons, she didn't care.

"It's no use," she said, wiggling her fingers through the holes in the grill. "There must be some kind of lock."

She worked her way around the edge of the grating, finally finding a block of cold steel jutting out.

"That's got to be it," Lina said. "Hold Crater's head."

Milo picked up the silver box as Lina reached for the tools in her belt.

"What are you going to do?" he asked.

Lina pulled her fusion torch out of its pouch. "Maybe nothing if this got too wet."

She pressed the button on the edge of the

small metal cylinder, but nothing happened. She gave it a shake and tried again. This time a tiny red energy blade shot forward.

"Can I borrow your visor?"

Milo passed his glasses to her. Covering her eyes, she plunged the tip of the torch into the grill on the other side of the lock. As she sliced through the metal, sparks rained down on her and acrid smoke began filling the pipe. Pushing her breathing mask over her mouth again, she slid the torch across the back of the lock and, with a crash, the grill clattered open.

Lina slipped the torch back into her belt and jumped down onto a small ledge that ran along the side of the sewer.

"Here, take this," Milo said, passing the silver box down to her before scrambling out of the pipe himself. Faint sunlight was streaming through grates in the ceiling high above. The sun was going down. They needed to move. It wouldn't be long before IG-70 and Rom came after them.

"There's some stairs," Milo said, edging his way along the ledge toward a ladder set into the brickwork. Lina followed, careful not to drop the silver box. She just hoped that Shalla was waiting for them up on the street.

Outside Twin Horns Storage, Shalla sat back on her speeder bike, stroking Morq's head. Something was wrong. The plan had been clear. Set off the alarm and grab the droid's head while everyone was outside. Then the children were supposed to return to the container and hide again. Shalla would barge into the reception, making a fuss that there had been an alarm and demanding her beetles back immediately. She'd walk out with the children safely hidden beneath the bugs. Simple.

But a second alarm had sent Odai and his henchmen running back into the building. Had the children been discovered?

Morq let out a worried squeal as the Mon

Calamari reappeared through the warehouse doors. He was shouting, telling his goons to "get them!" Shalla didn't have to ask who he was talking about. The Rodian and the assassin droid rushed around the side of the building with their weapons drawn.

Shalla backed her speeder into the shadows. Her fingers clenched around Morq's mane in frustration. The monkey-lizard yelped in pain as Shalla's lips drew back in a snarl.

Where *were* those kids?

CHAPTER 9
RESCUE

IN A DESERTED Lothal alleyway, Milo pushed aside a drain cover and climbed out. He turned around, reaching back down into the shaft to take the box containing CR-8R's head from his sister.

"Any sign of them?" Lina said as she pulled herself up into the alley.

Milo looked around. "Not yet, but they can't be far behind."

Just then, they heard the sound of running feet and the stomping of a heavy droid.

Milo grabbed Lina's hand and pulled her in the opposite direction.

"How are we going to find Shalla?" she said, chasing after him.

"We'll work that out when we're safe," Milo called.

"As if we're *ever* safe these days," Lina said with a sigh.

They made it to the end of the alleyway just as a speeder bike slid across the exit.

"Whoa!" Milo shouted as he almost crashed into the bike. "Watch it, Shalla!"

But it wasn't Shalla. The rider was a man with long brown hair and a full beard. The children took one look at him and turned around. But they were cut off by the silhouettes of Rom and IG-70 at the other end of the narrow lane.

They were trapped—again!

"Stay where you are!" the assassin droid boomed, taking a step into the alleyway.

"Yeah, where you are!" Rom repeated unhelpfully.

Milo squeezed his sister's hand. The guy on

the speeder must have worked for Odai, too. They were cornered!

"What are you waiting for?" the bearded man said. "Get on!"

Beside Milo, Lina turned around to face the speeder bike. "We haven't done anything wrong. Your boss stole Crater's head from *us*, remember!"

"My *boss*?" The man looked confused. "Don't you two want to be rescued?"

Milo's head snapped around. "Rescued?"

"Get on the bike!" the man said.

Milo's eyes went wide. There was something about the voice that he recognized, something familiar.

"You're the guy from the transmissions!"

"Yes, I am," the man said. "And if we don't move soon, I may never be able to make a transmission again!"

Milo raced forward, breaking Lina's hold on his hand. She paused but ran to the speeder bike as IG-70 shouted after them.

"You will wait!"

"No, we won't!" Milo yelled, jumping onto the bike as Lina climbed on behind him.

IG-70 was already shooting as the children's mysterious savior opened the throttle. The speeder bike shot forward, kicking up dust.

After weaving around buildings, the speeder bike finally came to a halt outside a nondescript building similar to the dozens they had already passed.

"Here we are," the man said, killing the bike's engine.

"We don't even know your name," Milo pointed out as he slid off the speeder.

"Inside," was the only reply as their rescuer swiped an ID card through a reader on the wall, opening a set of double doors.

Milo glanced at Lina, who shrugged. Neither of them knew if they should trust this guy. He turned back and sighed.

"Look, we can help you, but it isn't safe being on the streets right now. We need to get inside," he said.

"We?" Lina asked.

"Ephraim?" came a friendly but concerned female voice from inside.

"Don't worry, it's me," Ephraim replied. He nodded at Milo and Lina. "And I brought guests."

A woman appeared at the door. She was smaller than Ephraim and wore a purple headdress that matched her eyes.

"You found them," she said, beckoning to the children. "Come inside quickly."

Realizing they didn't have much choice, Milo led the way, still holding the box.

"We've been so worried about you," the woman said as Lina crossed the threshold, followed by Ephraim. The door closed behind him.

"You know who we are?" Lina asked.

"You were seen asking questions at the

landing strip," Ephraim explained, locking the door behind him. "It's just a pity you asked Cikatro Vizago."

"We've been following your signal, all the way from Thune," Lina told him.

Ephraim smiled. "It's reached that far, eh?"

Words spilled out of Milo's mouth. "Our parents were taken and we didn't know what to do, and then we heard your voice, and–"

"Hush, now," the woman said, walking to a table. "There's plenty of time for all that. Are you hungry? Do you need something to drink?"

Before they could answer, Milo heard a high-pitched giggle. It came from a cot on the other side of the room.

"You've got a baby!" he said, rushing over to see without asking.

"Milo!" Lina warned, but Ephraim laughed.

"It's fine. That's our son—Ezra."

Milo looked into the cot to see a chubby infant gazing up at him with big blue eyes. He had a mop of black hair and reached up with a pudgy arm.

Milo reached down and the baby wrapped a tiny hand around his finger. "He's cute."

"When he's not screaming his lungs out," the woman said with a laugh, joining them beside the crib. "My name's Mira, and you've already met my husband, Ephraim."

The bearded man held out his hand to Milo. "Ephraim Bridger. It's a pleasure to finally make your acquaintance. Sounds like you two have been through a lot."

Mira guided them toward the table and poured glasses of cold blue milk while they told their story.

⟨───⟩

"And your droid's head is in the box?" Ephraim asked when they'd finished recounting their narrow escape from Odai's lair.

Lina opened the box to remove CR-8R's head, gently stroking the droid's dormant face. "And our parents' secrets are in his head."

"If we'd known what you were getting into, we would have made contact sooner," Mira said sadly.

"But we had to be sure," Ephraim added. "We've been hearing more and more stories like yours—people being taken by Imperial forces and entire families disappearing."

"That's the reason we started our broadcasts," Mira told them. "To spread hope in these dark times. It was all we could think to do."

"And it worked," Lina said. "For us, at least. We followed your signal here."

"Because you hoped we could help track your parents?" Mira asked.

"Can you?" Lina asked.

The Bridgers looked at each other.

"It may not be as simple as that," Ephraim said.

"Why?"

"Show them," Mira said, placing a hand on her husband's arm.

Ephraim nodded and walked over to a circular couch in the corner. He pushed it aside to reveal an open hatch in the floor.

"You'll want to see this," he said, sitting on the edge of the hole and lowering himself onto a ladder. Milo and Lina crossed over to the hatch and looked down the deep shaft. Ephraim had reached the bottom. Milo didn't wait. Quickly, he climbed down.

"Wow!" he said, finding himself in a hidden

room packed with communication equipment. "Is this where you make the broadcasts?"

"And where we monitor Imperial channels, too," Ephraim confirmed, sitting in front of a large transmitter as Lina joined them. "The reason we were so careful is that we've heard that a bounty hunter is on Lothal." He pressed a control and a hologram appeared above the transmitter. It showed a masked figure. Its glowing eyes seemed to bore straight into Milo.

"Is that him?" Lina asked.

"He calls himself the Shade," Ephraim

replied. "No one knows what his face looks like behind the mask. We don't even know what's brought him to Lothal, other than it's something big. To be honest, we thought it might be us, but now that we know about your droid . . ."

"You think the Shade's looking for Mom and Dad's data?" Lina said.

"It's possible," Ephraim said. "I think we'd better get you off the planet."

"But we just got here," Milo said. "We need your help."

"We will help you," Mira reassured them. "We can ask around about your parents, but you'll be safer somewhere else, where the Shade can't find you."

"Can you tell us anything else about him?" Lina asked.

Ephraim looked doubtful. "The Shade? There isn't much to tell, other than the fact that he's one of the most dangerous bounty hunters in the Outer Rim. There was something the other day, though." He continued working the controls, scrolling through files on a screen. "A deep-space camera picked up an image that could potentially be the Shade's ship, heading this way from Kessel."

"From Kessel?" Lina asked, frowning.

Ephraim nodded. "The spice mine planet." He found what he was looking for. "Here it is."

He pressed a button and the hologram changed. The Shade was replaced by a blurry picture of a speeding freighter in space.

Milo felt his stomach drop.

"What is it?" Ephraim asked, noticing that the color had drained from Milo's face. "Do you recognize the ship?"

Milo's mouth was dry and he couldn't believe what he was seeing. "Yeah, I do." He turned to his sister. "Lina, isn't that the *Moveable Feast*?"

CHAPTER 10
THE GETAWAY

AT TWIN HORNS STORAGE, Cikatro Vizago was getting tired of Odai yelling at him.

"Where are they?" Rask Odai ranted. "How long could it possibly take to find two children?"

"I'm on this, okay?" Vizago said, holding a communicator to his lips. "Rom? IG-70? Come in, please. The boss wants a word!"

"A word? I just want my head back!" Odai snapped.

"Sounds like you're losing your head to me," Vizago muttered under his breath.

"What was that?"

"Nothing, boss," the Devaronian said, talking

into the communicator again. "Rom! IG-70! Where are you?"

"Cikatro Vizago," a woman said. The horned alien turned to see Shalla Mondatha strolling into the warehouse.

He tried to wave the woman away. "Not now, okay? Your bugs are safe, but we're closed." He turned his back on her and called for Rom and IG-70 one last time.

"I don't think they can hear you," Shalla said, and Vizago jumped as something heavy thudded at his feet. A tall cylinder rolled across the floor, coming to rest in front of him.

It was IG-70's mechanical head with scorched wires hanging from its neck.

Vizago spun around to find Shalla pointing an energy bow in his direction.

"Where are the children?" she said.

"What do you think you're doing?" Odai raged beside Vizago. He was not used to having his henchman threatened in their establishment.

"Asking a question," Shalla replied coolly. "A question I asked your Rodian and assassin droid a few minutes ago. They answered incorrectly. I suggest you tell me what I want to know."

"And what's that?" Vizago asked, wondering how quickly he could draw Vilmarh's Revenge.

"The man on the speeder bike, the one who took the children—who is he?" Shalla asked.

"We have no idea what you're talking about!" Odai gurgled.

"Wrong answer," Shalla said, swinging her bow around to shoot one of the golden droids behind the front desk. It exploded in a shower of sparks.

Her weapon was pointing at Vizago again in the blink of an eye.

"We want to find those kids as much as you do," the Devaronian said. He narrowed his eyes. "Unless . . . you know something about the robbery!"

"It was you," Odai spluttered. "You were in on it!"

Shalla rolled her eyes. "This is taking too long."

She twisted again, zapping the second droid. Vizago took his chance. He reached for Vilmarh's Revenge. But before he could even slip the blaster from its holster, Shalla had swung her bow toward him and fired.

Vizago screamed as he was thrown back, Vilmarh's Revenge skidding across the floor. His hand shot up to his left horn. The tip was missing! The woman had blown it clean off!

Now Shalla was pointing her bow at Odai. The Mon Calamari was showing his true colors. He sniveled behind the front desk like the cowardly bully he was.

"Don't shoot," he begged. "I'll tell you whatever you want to know, just don't shoot."

"That's better." Shalla smiled cruelly. "Now, I'm going to ask you one more time. Who took the children?"

"You know him?" Ephraim spluttered. "You know the Shade?"

"Not him," Milo said. "*Her*. Captain Shalla Mondatha. She's running some kind of café down at the landing strip."

"A *café*?" Ephraim said skeptically.

"It must be a cover," Lina said.

Ephraim rubbed his hand against his beard. "And a good one, too. What better way to get people talking than by feeding them? There's no such thing as a free lunch, after all."

Lina looked down at her jumpsuit. "That's why she had all the equipment for the heist. She said it was because she used to be a smuggler."

"But she's really a bounty hunter," said Milo. "Sent to find us!"

"But why not just grab you when she had the chance?" Ephraim mused. "Why go through with the robbery?"

"Because it's not us she wants," Milo said.

"The data in Crater's head!" Lina said. "That's why she was helping us. Oh, we're so stupid!"

She thrust her hand into a pocket, pulling out the visor she'd borrowed from Milo in the sewer.

"This thing can transmit," Lina said. "That's how she sent us the picture of the keypad."

"What if it can track as well?" Milo asked.

Ephraim took the visor from her, examining it closely. He sighed. "You're right. There's a tracker built in."

"Then she knows we're here!" Milo exclaimed.

Ephraim shook his head. "Not necessarily." He looked around the small room. "This place is shielded."

"To protect your messages?" Lina guessed. Ephraim nodded.

"That's the idea. Our signal is bounced around the local datanet before being broadcast, rather than transmitting direct from our home."

"So the Empire can't trace the transmission back to the source," Lina said, completing Ephraim's explanation. "Clever."

"And your shield will disrupt the Shade's tracker?" Milo asked.

Ephraim didn't look so sure. "For now at

least. It's not perfect though. The longer you stay here . . ."

"The more likely it is that she'll find us."

Lina sighed. "Then we need to go."

"I didn't say that," Ephraim insisted.

"No," Lina argued. "But it's true. We can't put you in danger because of us. What you're doing is too important."

"And you have Ezra, too," Milo added.

Lina made a decision. "We need to get back to the *Whisper Bird* and take off as soon as possible."

"As long as we have enough fuel," Milo said. "Plus, if Shalla's tracking the visor . . ."

"Then let her follow it," Ephraim said, grabbing a tool from the table. As the children watched, he pressed it into the side of the glasses, a signal beeping on his transmitter. "Yes, I thought so."

He adjusted a control on the transmitter and a holographic map of Capital City appeared in the air, a tiny dot flashing.

"Transmissions work two ways," he explained. "That's the Shade, looking for you. Now, if I take this visor over to the other side of town, she'll come running. She'll follow me, not you."

"While we head back to the *Whisper Bird*," Lina said. "But won't that put you in the line of fire?"

"Don't worry about Ephraim," Mira called down from the top of the ladder. "He was a bit of a speed demon when he was younger. He can outrace anyone."

Ephraim led them back up into the lounge. "I'm just sorry we can't do more. Once you get away, we'll start looking for your parents and be in touch."

"You should take this, too," Mira said, pushing a bag into Lina's hands. "To buy more fuel. I'm just sorry it's not more."

Lina looked inside. It was full of credits. "We can't take this."

"You can, and you have to. Do you know the way back to the landing strip from here?"

Lina nodded as Milo grabbed CR-8R's head. "I think so."

"Then we need to go," Ephraim said, nodding toward the door. "It's dark out there, but the moons should give you enough light. You need to get off Lothal as soon as you can!"

Neither Lina nor Milo spoke as they ran along the Lothal streets. They tried to stay in the long shadows cast by the skyscrapers. The tall towers didn't look so beautiful anymore.

They stopped with every transport that passed, darting into doorways and behind stalls. It was hard not to imagine Shalla jumping out of them at every turn.

No, not Shalla. The Shade. They didn't even know if Shalla was her real name.

The *Whisper Bird* was waiting for them when they made it to the landing strip. The *Moveable Feast* was still next to it, but the Shade's craft was closed. There was no light blazing through its portholes.

Clutching CR-8R's head, Milo raced for the *Bird*, only stopping when he heard an excited cry. He turned to see Morq crouched below a nearby speeder bike.

"There you are," Milo said, running to his pet. "I was scared she'd hurt you. Come on, we need to get on board the *Bird*."

Morq didn't move. He just sat there, quivering.

"What's wrong with him?" Lina asked as she came up behind Milo. That was when she noticed the collar around Morq's thin neck. It was connected to a chain tied around the speeder bike.

"I wondered if you'd come back for him," came a voice from behind them. It was Shalla, standing beneath the nose of the *Whisper Bird*. She was still wearing her knitted shawl, but now it was covering black body armor instead of overalls.

"I suppose I don't need this anymore," she said, unfastening the shawl at her neck. "You don't look very pleased to see me."

"We know who you are!" Lina shouted back, standing next to her brother. "You're a bounty hunter—the Shade!"

"Am I now?" Shalla asked, turning the shawl inside out. The other side of the fabric was dark and smooth, like a cloak. She draped it over her shoulders again, fixing the clasp beneath her chin.

"Where's your mask?" Milo asked, trying to sound threatening. Lina wasn't sure it had worked.

Shalla cocked her head. "I can put it on if you want. Maybe after you've given me that droid."

"No," Lina said, moving to stand in front of Milo. "We won't."

"I thought you'd say that." Shalla smiled. "It was clever, ditching the visor. Whoever rescued you obviously still thinks I'm chasing it around town."

"We found your signal," Lina insisted.

"No, you found a tracker stuck to the back of a Wakizan beetle. As soon as I realized that Odai didn't have you, I knew you'd come back for your ship. So I prepared a little welcome home surprise for you." Shalla pulled out a gloved hand. She was holding her datapad. "Either you surrender, or I press this button."

"And what will that do?" Milo asked.

"Oh, nothing much," Shalla said. "Just detonate the thermo-grenade I've hidden on that speeder bike. You know, the one chained to your little pet!"

Milo turned to look at Morq, who was staring at them with wide, frightened eyes. "You can't! He hasn't done anything to you!"

"I can and I will," Shalla insisted. "So what's it going to be, Milo? Surrender or say bye-bye, Morq."

Ephraim Bridger pulled up alongside the landing strip, killing his speeder bike's engines.

It had quickly become clear that the Shade wasn't following him, so he had taken the fight to her, tracking her signal to an alleyway not far from Twin Horns Storage.

He'd eventually found the tracker stud on the back of a particularly nasty-looking insect. She'd tricked them.

But maybe the children had reached their ship before she'd found them. Maybe they'd gotten away. He would check the landing strip and then get back to Mira. There was only one problem. He had no idea what their ship looked like.

There was one he recognized though—the *Moveable Feast*.

The Shade's ship.

A sudden movement caught his eye. Someone was walking from behind the birdlike ship next to the *Feast*.

His heart sank when he saw who it was.

Milo and Lina Graf were being led toward

the *Feast* by a figure in a long cloak. Ephraim pulled out a pair of electrobinoculars and took a closer look. It was a woman, with CR-8R's head tucked underneath her arm. He checked the *Feast*'s ramp, spotting a droid's headless body already loaded on the ship.

He lowered the binoculars. Could he stop them before they took off?

It was doubtful. Even if he moved quickly,

there was no guarantee that the Shade wouldn't hurt the children. Besides, Ephraim was no fighter. He knew that.

But he had friends who were.

Grimly, he watched as the party marched up the ramp. It raised with the sound of hydraulic gears, and seconds later, the *Feast*'s engines roared. A cloud of dirt billowed from beneath the freighter as it rose into the air. A moment later, it swept overhead and blasted high into the sky.

Ephraim pulled a communicator from his tunic and opened a channel.

"Ryder, it's me. . . . Yes, I know you told me not to call you just yet, but this is important. We need to mount a rescue. . . ."

TO BE CONTINUED IN
STAR WARS
ADVENTURES IN WILD SPACE
Book Four: THE DARKNESS